BODIES of WATER

BODIES of WATER

short fiction by
ROSANNE CASH

HYPERION

new york

Library of Congress Cataloging-In-Publication Data

Cash, Rosanne.
Bodies of water: short fiction/by Rosanne Cash.—1st ed.
p. cm.
ISBN 0-7868-6083-9
1. Manners and customs—Fiction. I. Title.
PS3553.A39375B63 1996
813'.54— dc20
95–44148 CIP

Book Design by Claudyne Bianco Bedell

First Edition

10 9 8 7 6 5 4 3 2 1

for my children

contents

BODIES of WATER

WE ARE BORN

We were looking for a Christmas tree in a little makeshift tree lot next to a department store when I felt the first contraction. I went slowly up and down the rows of pine and spruce behind my husband and my girls, nodding yes, shrugging maybe, as they pointed out their choices. All the while my abdomen was squeezing me with an intensity that felt as if it would like to separate my body into two halves. I was surprised that it was so powerful, so early. I didn't say anything to them, wanting to be sure.

We chose a sweet-smelling Douglas fir and made our way home to thaw our frozen toes and fingers in front of a modest fire, prop the tree in a metal bucket, and dig out the boxes of ornaments. The pains were getting stronger. I went upstairs to lie down, and after a few more contractions, came back down to the living room.

"I'm in labor," I panted to my husband. My doctor, a sweet and shy young man, had been gently adamant that he would induce labor the very next day if it had not occurred naturally by then. I had been anxious about this for the past week, fearing that a whole generation of artificially induced babies would for their entire lives be psychologically out of step with themselves because of their forced entries into the world. When I reached him on the phone the doctor told me to come to the hospital immediately. I asked if I might spend just the afternoon at home, but he was firm. I didn't argue: She was my third baby, she was nearly two weeks overdue and I was already in a lot of pain. My husband and I called the babysitter, got my bag, and drove silently to the hospital.

• • •

ROSANNE CASH

I am running across a field, past the grape arbor, past the peach orchard, through the tall yellow grass that shimmers in the dry California heat near my grandparents' little white clapboard house. I am eleven years old. I can see the railroad tracks ahead and I can feel the rails on the ground before I even reach them. The smooth, warm steel under my bare feet connects me to the earth, lets me know I'm really here. With all my cells and breath and sweat I just want to get to the tracks. My grandmother is inside the house behind me, baking Scripture cake, which uses only ingredients found in the Bible. The ingredients themselves are listed in her recipe by citation to each relevant chapter and verse, so someone less knowledgeable and virtuous than my grandmother would have to get out her Bible and look them all up. My grandma, however, knows them all by heart.

My grandfather is in the grape arbor, as always tugging at the trousers that bunch up at his crotch, smoking an endless series of hand-rolled cigarettes.

My parents are gone, not for good, but

they have been in the newspaper, and I have seen it, and something of them is gone for good. I keep running to keep the thing that has vanished from making my chest hurt and my eyes fill with water. I run as if I would never stop. I run because I can almost see myself as an adult, and the murky vision terrifies me. I run because in the world in which I live, men are regarded to be irredeemably selfish and cruel, and women to be unfailingly virtuous. I run because I know I can never truly take my place in that picture.

My husband had stopped shaving on her due date and announced that he would not shave again until she was born. By the time we went to the hospital, a dark, scruffy little beard had grown around his angular face, and circles from the sleepless nights of waiting and not knowing had formed under his blue eyes. As we settled into our mauve and gray hotel-tasteful hospital room, he slipped on a T-shirt that advertised the hotel in Santa Monica where we had conceived this baby during a night of wild lovemaking the previous spring. We had been to an industry conference that night, and after several tedious hours of handshaking and tight little smiles and then a bottle of red wine, we had been ready to let off some steam.

In my hospital room now, I prop up the macramé god's-eyes my girls have made for me as focal objects. When the contractions become too strong and my breathing becomes erratic, I can stare at these blue and red popsicle-stick-and-yarn inventions and find a hole through the blur of pain.

I am really having this baby, I tell myself, after nearly a month of false labor and three disappointing trips to the hospital. I had forgotten how much a contraction actually hurt. I struggled to make myself comfortable. I was nearly two hundred pounds of woman and baby and excess water packed into a five-foot-five-inch frame. It was a challenge.

My doctor came in and put his hand up inside me, apparently unconcerned that several nurses had already done so and reported their findings to him. I had been four centimeters dilated to a tall nurse with big hands; five centimeters to a little nurse with small fingers. He announced that I was between four and five centimeters. I arched my eyebrows in mock surprise and genuine relief as he let his hand slip out.

The yellow grass reaches to my waist and makes me feel small but protected, an experience I have not had since I was three. The steel tracks warm my toes and my soul there in the silence of that summer day. No one would follow me here. I feel almost at home with myself, safe enough to let my thoughts wander. Earlier in that week, before my parents appeared in the newspaper, I had gathered peaches from the orchard in baskets of a dozen or so, and arranged them for sale on a table near the front lawn of the clapboard house. I offered them for a dollar a basket, but it was hard even to give them away, the area was so overgrown with ancient peach orchards. If I was lucky, I might sell one basket in a day. When I got frustrated with the peach business, I made a tall pitcher of lemonade and sold it for a nickel a glass. It was a hot summer, and I was near a busy road, but the cars seldomed slowed, even when I yelled at them as they swooped past me.

The white clapboard house and the grape arbor and the peach orchard were adjacent to a little trailer park, which my grandparents managed. I loved to patrol the rows of trailers and grew to know who was friendly toward children and who didn't want to be bothered. My favorite tenant was a new bride of nineteen and her perpetually absent husband. She had a ten-month-old baby boy whom she treated casually but lovingly—a style of parenting I had never before witnessed. I never saw her husband in the trailer and never questioned her about him, but I thrilled whenever she referred to him in conversation. I was fascinated by her autonomy, her youth, and her strangely confident image of herself in her role as a wife and mother. She considered me a friend, and I was deeply flattered by her attention and lack of condescension.

One day that summer I went to visit her and pounded on her door for fifteen minutes or more until she opened, never thinking that a grown-up, especially a mother, might be asleep at ten o'clock in the morning. She finally came to the door bleary-eyed and with an intense headache. I was surprised and confused. I didn't hear the baby inside. I backed down her front steps, apologizing awkwardly. I rode my bike slowly away, not understanding the feeling of complete despair that overtook me.

I never visited her trailer after that day. With a self-negating kind of sixth sense, I had chosen to idealize an image of womanhood in the shape of a girl who bitterly reminded me, with a feeling that sickened my stomach but that I was afraid to examine more closely, that I would never be good enough, and that the world inside my head and body was a square peg to the round hole of my ancestral imprinting. I looked for company elsewhere in the trailer park but, disheartened and defensive, finally gave up on my quest, and the peach orchard, and the lemonade stand altogether.

· · ·

ROSANNE CASH

I was twenty-four when my first baby was born, twenty-six when the second came; perhaps the perfect physical age to give birth. I'm now thirty-four. My body is reeling, searching for the cellular memory that will enlighten me as to how to accomplish this. I have waves of soggy panic rising in my chest, fueled by each contraction, creating a resistance that causes the next contraction to be even more excruciating. Fourteen hours have passed. This pain fills the room, rattles the windows, drips down the walls, crushes me back into my pillows, dampens the sheets, and creates an acrid smell in my nostrils. I am amazed that my husband and the nurses don't feel it, see it, or smell it; this incredible force is actually contained entirely within my body. I have wrestled it, ridden it, been transformed by it, and now I've had enough. I ask for an anesthetic.

As I wait for a doctor to bring the injection, I fix my eyes on the little god's-eyes propped on a shelf on the far wall, paralyzing myself in defense of the pain. The energy of other people, their words and their touch upon my skin, break the charged field around me, weaken my intent, and irritate me beyond belief. With my eyes closed, I am aware of my husband's hand even as he just begins to lift it and reach toward me, two feet above my body. "Don't touch me," I beg, and, as I push his caresses away, I also struggle against the nurse as she fusses with the fetal monitor strapped to my enormous abdomen.

The anesthesiologist finally arrives with a needle to insert into my spine. He asks me to sit up and dangle my feet over the side of the bed. My husband and the nurse pull me to a sitting position. The doctor pauses with the needle poised in the air and stares at me indifferently.

"You can't move a muscle while I do this," he says flatly. "And it's going to hurt."

I am seized with a sudden and profound hatred for his entire gender. My mouth tastes like warm metal, like the needle he is about to stick in my back.

"It's going to hurt," I repeat calmly, more as a statement than a question. He lowers his hand to my spine. "You can give it to me with an ice pick, for all I care," I say under my breath, and close my eyes as he inserts the needle between two vertebrae low in my back, just as a powerful contraction hits me full force, with no warning, no build-up. I breathe, I let the tears escape through the corners of my eyes, I squeeze the hand of my husband who is kneeling between my legs, who is now the one man I don't hate, and I don't move a muscle. The drug takes effect, and I slowly lay back on my damp pillows. My husband sends out for frozen yogurt.

The summer I was eleven I felt too big for my body, too small for my heart, confused by the secrets and fears that permeated the very atoms of the air inside my home, and far too old for my age. I was not just mother to my mother and sisters; at times I felt grandmother to them. I tried playing at being a child, but I tired of it and became sarcastic. I remember thinking clearly, at eleven, that if I was expected to be so mature at such a young age, then I did not wish to wear ankle socks anymore. They didn't go with my life.

I can close my eyes and see myself with the grass waving around my waist, my bare feet edging to the tracks to feel the warm metal soak into my soles. I see myself on the day that began this pivotal year, my eleventh birthday, standing next to my mother's prize rosebush as she takes my picture with a six-inch white bloom she has placed delicately between my fingers. I have this photograph, today, in a little silver frame on my nightstand: an odd and pathetic relic. The look of sardonic embarrassment on my puffy, shut-down, girl-with-a-birthday face tells the whole story: What exactly was being captured on film? Me, as I turned eleven, or the spectacular six-inch bloom?

When I was eleven, I stopped dreaming the dreams that didn't come true, I stopped talking to people who didn't listen, I lost hope and I retreated. I assumed that the root of the problem was that I was too strange for the real world. That being the case, I created a charming and dynamic personality to make the necessary forays into the Outside, and I kept my strangeness for myself; my own peculiar jewels under lock and key.

ROSANNE CASH

· · ·

Twenty-three-and-a- half years later I am pushing a baby out of my body with all the strength I have left after an interminable twenty hours of labor. She is stuck; I am stuck. I am exhausted and crying. I can no longer lift myself off the pillows to help push, so my husband and a nurse lift me and force my legs open. My doctor says he needs to intervene. The baby has been in the birth canal too long, and it is becoming too stressful for her. He gently pushes a suction cup inside me and attaches it to the top of her head. He pulls with my next push, and she slides out and cries. The poor battered creature is as ravaged as I am. She has been squeezed so tightly inside me that all the blood vessels in her right eye have burst, and it is brilliant red where it should be white. She is swollen and bruised, and the most luminous being I have ever seen. I take her onto my stomach, so weak I am afraid I will drop her, but exhilarated and proud. My blood, which covers her tiny body, smears my stomach and arms, but I hold and stroke her in this sticky mess until we are both peaceful. Her father cradles her and adores her, and her sisters come in, tentative but smiling, and take her in their arms. The room is humid with our power.

Several hours later, when everyone has gone home and she and I are alone just before dawn in the dark room, I take her from her bassinette and place her in my bed. I construct a barricade of pillows behind her and place a heating pad beneath her stomach. I ease myself onto my side and stroke her little head and watch her sleep. We are in a silent and immaculate world, distant from all things common. We are still in the realm of miracles. She, so newly arrived from that plane of existence where everything is known and all things are possible, vibrates with a perfection I can only vaguely remember in my most vulnerable states, but which deeply stirs me. At this moment, she embodies and bequeaths infinite knowledge, she gives me access to myself and to the God who helped arrange this. I drift in this altered state with her, my body bruised and beyond exhaustion, my spirit fed by her very presence and by our grand, mutual achievement. Her name has not yet been decided, so I whisper to her in the dark, "What is your name, darling?" And a voice in my ear, the voice that belonged to the dead child who was me, whispers back, "I have one, too."

Everything is clear now, for this one stark moment. The past rushes to meet me. This unknown soul who has used my body as a vehicle to enter this world has come to heal not only herself but me as well. I am shattered, but the pieces form a whole. The dead have returned, gently, and without rancor, she and I. The grass will wave around my waist again and forever, my soul will fit my body and contain my heart, and there will be warm steel under my feet and not in my mouth. The ancestral wives and mothers are losing their grip on me; it is slipping away with every breath of this newborn goddess who sleeps on a heating pad in my bed. I will learn to dance and command the newly charged atoms of my childhood home, which I have carried inside me for so long. I will dream the dreams that come true and I will not be afraid of them. I will stand next to a rose, and not be overshadowed. I have given birth, and we are born.

THE ARC OF LONELINESS

The arc of loneliness curves suddenly into view at the oddest moments: when by chance I see the unknown woman who lives in the apartment across the street through her living room window, adjusting the knick-knacks on her mantle; when a stranger in rough clothing passes me on the sidewalk smelling of cigarettes and spearmint chewing gum, which makes me think of suicide. Not my own, not even his, necessarily, just suicide, another segment on the arc. There is no present time on the arc, only past and future, those most frustrating limbos of thought. Deferred pain is the drug of choice—feeling seen in a mirror, framed by calculation and distance. Deferred pain is the heat that shapes the arc.

One day there is nothing left to do but go away to an island. On the plane, an eight-year old with an excess of testosterone keeps running across my feet. Finally I grab him by his T-shirt and say, very sweetly, "Listen, darling, if you don't stop trampling me I'm going to make you sit on my lap while I tell you my entire life story. Including a lot of details about drug rehab and my divorce." He goes back to his seat.

On the island, sitting on a tiled terrace, with the smell of wild orchids making me absolutely dizzy, listening to a million different birds sing and waves breaking in the near distance, I find I can think only of one thing: *Serial monogamy: biological imperative or excuse for failure?* I am continually distracted by contemplation of this, or similar questions. A vacation is of no use to me. A jetliner bound for a holiday just sails the curve of the arc, like a heat-seeking missile bound to find the deferred pain.

These are the thoughts that soothe me when I am encircled in this arc: that perhaps I am already a ghost to some dear relation centuries away. Perhaps something I have recently done is now disturbing her future equilibrium. She is surely someone I would love, and rattling her from my place in the past is my way to know her. We connect.

My distruptive rhythms are even now rippling through time and my own gene pool. It is comforting to become the crazy ancestor. I am a brooding face staring from a old painting in a stranger's house, a stranger who has my blood. My memories of the future are not nightmares, but a product of the deepest longing, to want what doesn't yet exist, to miss those who have not yet been born. The future is the point on the curve of the arc just where it bends out of view.

. . .

My legs have been numb for thirty years. They have clenched the arc as if it were an oiled saddle attached to nothing. We have ridden it to exhaustion. As I step off and survey my surroundings, an occasional but necessary foray, I find my skills at relating to other human beings are nonexistent, desperately lacking, or rusty at best. Too many years saddled to a phantom stallion. I am now waiting for my legs to come to life and inform my whole body of the appropriate next move.

My daughter goes to nursery school. She tells me on our walk there one morning that every day after she is dropped off, she gets a funny feeling of missing-me-and-being-worried. I describe the feeling for her in detail, invent some memories of when my own mother left me at nursery school and how my fears gradually turned to excitement at the various opportunities for learning and play, and assure her that she will soon feel the same. What I don't tell her is that I have the identical gnawing anxiety when I leave her in the morning, and usually linger at the window to watch her. It is unbearable to let go. One afternoon, having come a little early to pick her up, I watched her on the playground through the fence from the street. She was arguing loudly with another five-year-old girl. I was stunned. She is the most gentle, soft-hearted child ever to breathe, and yet she was standing with clenched fists, telling the other child exactly what she thought of her in a loud, trembling voice. The other little girl stared at her implacably. My daughter turned away angrily and walked to a bush, where she buried her face and sobbed loudly. She buried her face in a bush to cry. What a great idea, I thought; so poetic. She is an artist. It is a sublime torment to receive the unfathomable gift of her confidences and her innocent dependence. I don't trust myself with such munificence; I, who don't give a bush a second glance. In those moments, I stumble back to the arc. I mount the saddled ghost. I wave to her from afar.

ACTING SCHOOL

When I was in acting school I met a girl in my cold-reading class who happened to live in the same apartment building as I did. She had a remarkably voluptuous figure, and she always wore her blond hair in a ponytail on the right side of her head. She favored lipstick the shade of fluorescent blood. I can't remember her name now, but I do remember that she once borrowed three dollars from me to buy champagne. I didn't ask what kind of champagne she intended to buy with three dollars, because this happened the day after we met, and I thought it might be too personal a question. So I just gave it to her.

I lived on the first floor, and she lived on the third, and she often appeared unannounced at my door for a little chat. In the year and a half that I knew her, I never saw her sit on a chair or sofa. She had an odd habit of squatting on her heels in a corner of the room, and carried on conversations perched in this way for a half hour or more. She said she had seen it done in the Orient and she thought it looked elegant. Even then, with my limited ability to analyze character, I thought she was unbearably pretentious. I defiantly sat on the sofa, waiting for her thigh muscles to implode.

She had a rich boyfriend who traveled frequently to South America on business. Their apartment was filled with South American art and artifacts, carvings, paintings, and photos. She looked oddly mismatched with the primitive art, as if someone had drawn Betty Boop into a corner of a Frida Kahlo painting.

Once, when I had been invited up to her place, she showed me a bunch of dead roses on her bedside table that her rich boyfriend had sent her from Brazil about six months earlier.

She couldn't wait to tell me exactly how much it had cost to send flowers from one hemisphere to the next. Then she confided breathlessly that she was concerned that our acting teacher would be offended by her body odor in our morning session because she liked to make love in the mornings and was loath to shower after sex, preferring to go sweaty and sticky from bed straight to sensory class. I was terribly embarrassed by this confession and couldn't imagine that she would even consider bringing it up with our teacher, which she did, the next day.

One late afternoon when a warm desert wind was blowing around on my patio, she came downstairs for an impromptu visit and squatted regally by the sliding door. I could see the leaves and the dust dancing through the glass behind her ponytail. She had an annoying habit of sucking in her breath sharply just before she spoke, as if everything she said startled her in advance.

(Sharp intake of breath) "I just gave forty dollars to one of the bag ladies on Hollywood Boulevard."

I was stunned. And suspicious. "What? You did? That's a lot of money."

She lifted her head and stuck out her chin. (Gasp) "Yes, I know. I can do without moisturizer for a month," she replied airily.

I didn't know what to say. I knew I was far more selfless than she, and I couldn't do without moisturizer for a month. Whatever she was trying to prove made me suddenly very tired.

Perhaps I should describe myself at this point in my life. I was twenty-two years old, and my feet were a little too big for my body. I was slightly overweight, and I had recently gotten a perm that was still far too tight. I was excruciatingly self-conscious, and I suspected that everyone knew something very important that I hadn't been clued in on. I had dreams about being chased once or twice a week. I spent almost all my time at acting school and I never ate a proper meal. I had two things in my refrigerator: a bottle of Perrier and an open can of tuna fish.

I had two cats—a serious mistake—as I had been looking for an image and thought they might help. I got them from the animal shelter, and as soon as they passed the kitten stage, an anxious feeling came over me and with every passing day I realized more and more how profoundly I did not want cats in my life. I had named them after my imaginary childhood friends, and I grew to deeply regret this infringement on my memories. When I was alone in my apartment with them I sometimes became overwhelmed by their felineness and locked them in the bathroom.

My upstairs friend wasn't aware of my dark and secret compulsions toward my cats, of course. When she ventured downstairs she took us at face value: a disturbed, curly-haired, overweight cat-loving drama student and her two rather highstrung kitties. She, on the other hand, was blatantly gorgeous, marginally talented, redolent of sex, unfathomably self-confident, and wore her dramatic little airs as if they were Chanel No. 5.

Our relationship went on like this for several months: me, a perpetually intrigued but mostly silent audience, she, theatrical and patronizing in her exclusive living room performances.

Then I met a man to whom I was enormously attracted. Andrew, a dark-haired, blue eyed actor, was in my improv class. One night he improvised a guard at Buckingham Palace. He never moved a muscle for an entire half hour. By the end of the thiry minutes, the entire class, including myself, was on the floor, doubled up in laughter. Tears were streaming down my face. He didn't budge; not a shadow of an expression crossed his face. The more we laughed, the more he didn't move. I knew then that he was the man for me, but I thought he'd never notice me in a million years.

After class that very night he approached me and asked if I was free the following evening. I was free, to say the very least.

The next afternoon, I spent nearly two hours deciding on an outfit that would look as if the subject of clothing had never crossed my mind, but would in fact show off my best features and miraculously hide the extra pounds. I took another hour trying to blow-dry half of the curl out of my hair. I let the cats out of the bathroom just before he arrived. I even held one of them casually in the crook of my arm as I opened the door.

With unnerving ease he strode into my apartment and glanced around. He spied the other cat, which had taken its desultory place on the sofa. "How many cats do you have?" he asked.

"Two," I said, and gave him what I hoped was my best earth-goddess/friend-to-all-creatures smile.

"I never have liked cats," he said, eyeing the one in my arms a little distastefully, but smiling gently. "I don't know what it is."

I let the cat drop from my arm, and rallied. "I haven't had them very long, actually. These are my first cats. They're kind of an experiment," I said, feeling my hair getting curlier by the second. We walked into the kitchen and stood talking, and then, at a pause in the conversation, he absentmindedly reached over and opened my refrigerator. I stared at the floor, paralyzed with horror. I felt my buttons pop, my feet grow, and my shaky persona collapse. He frowned at my Perrier and my pathetic can of tuna fish, and then sighed deeply. He slowly closed the refrigerator door.

"Would you like to go to dinner?" he asked sweetly.

Three nights later, burglars paid a visit to my apartment building. Andrew and I were standing on the patio, enjoying the evening breeze and the giddy implications of our second date in less than a week, when we noticed two men with crowbars in the shadows at the front entrance.

"There was a break-in three doors down last night! These must be the same guys. I'm calling the police," I whispered, tripping over myself as I rushed to the phone.

Andrew leaned languidly against the railing on propped elbows, watching the burglars attempting to break in.

"Are they still there?" I called from inside, staring at the round curve of his butt through the glass door. There had been no sex yet.

"Yes. But they're not in yet."

I got the police on the line, told them there was a break-in in progress, and gave them my address. I hurried back to the patio, just in time to hear the sharp crack of wood splintering. Two figures slipped through the open doorway.

"They're in," we both whispered at the same time.

"Come on," Andrew said and took my arm. "We should get out of your apartment. Let's go out the back way to the front of the building and wait for the police."

We stood together awkwardly in the middle of the street for the few minutes it took the squad car to come squealing toward us. Andrew flagged it down and pointed to my building. As the car screeched to a halt, two cops jumped out, grabbed Andrew, and slammed him up against the side of the car.

"No, no, no!" I moved quickly to his side. "He's not the burglar! He's my friend! I'm the one who called!"

They looked at me narrowly. The taller of the two had Andrew's arm pinned behind his back.

"What are you doing in the street?" he asked accusingly.

"We were waiting for you!" I said, stammering. The cop let him go with reluctance. Andrew rubbed his arm.

"Hey, thanks," he said and turned toward me with an amused smile.

I moved close to him. He suddenly put his arms around me, nearly lifted me from the ground, and kissed me firmly and damply on the mouth.

My toes were suddenly tingling and my chest was hot. For a brief moment, I forgot why I was in the street. I looked at the police. Did I call them here to witness this kiss? I shook myself a little. They obviously wanted information. I was not the least interested, but I roused myself sufficiently to make a pretense of sober good citizenship. "They had, uh, crowbars and they broke in the front door." I explained, looking at Andrew.

At this very moment my upstairs neighbor arrived home in her red sportscar, her blond ponytail swaying, her red lips pursed. She stopped directly in front of Andrew and me and gasped. For once, it sounded appropriate.

ROSANNE CASH

"What the HELL is going on?" she demanded through her rolled-down window.

"Burglars," I said. The police were moving indoors, although the tall one was glancing back regretfully at her.

"Well," she sucked in her breath and dropped her voice, "who's that?" She nodded toward Andrew as she opened the car door.

As I introduced them, she arched her back slightly and settled more deeply into her hips. An awards-show smile played around her florid mouth.

"Hi. I live upstairs." Little intakes of breath dotted her every word.

Andrew raised his eyebrows slightly, then knit them close together. Her mouth was so unnaturally bright that it appeared to move around her face randomly. I was transfixed at the illusion of her migrating lips, but her tight stovepipe jeans with the little zippers at the ankles were suddenly laughable. Her ponytail was bobbing like a plastic dog on the dashboard of an old Chevy. When she struck her I-dreamed-I-won-an-Oscar-in-my-Maidenform-bra pose, her curves seemed as if they were drawn on with crayon by an unsteady hand. Her affectations ceased to intrigue me with an almost audible thud. I felt wonderful and raw. I felt liberated from my hair, my body, my fear. I don't know what happened in those few seconds, but I was aware that I wasn't wondering if he was responding to her, I wasn't sizing myself up next to her, I wasn't reaching or holding. I was just there, under a starlit, dry, and breezy evening adjacent to the scene of a crime, removed from my past and freed from the future it would have led to.

Now, many years later, when I find myself desperate with the need to order the way he loves me, when I find myself eaten up with doubt, unable to live inside my own skin, I long for a night like that, a night so clear that it seems the stars and the wind are alive with melodies to accompany my inner epiphanies.

The burglars have long since disappeared. It has been twelve years since that night. As I recall, only one third-floor apartment, full of South American relics and dead roses, was broken into, and my ponytailed friend took a tall, happy policeman upstairs to her newly pristine quarters to have a gorgeous little fit and file a lengthy police report enhancing the particulars of her indiguation with three-dollar champagne, I have no doubt. Andrew stayed the night, and we took our first tentative steps into what would be an extravagant and challenging romance. I have been ever aware that we began with a break-in. The very next day, I put an ad in the newspaper: "Two young male cats. Troubled history; need good home. Free."

BODIES OF WATER

This is what I do: I wake up in a hotel—a nice hotel, orchids in the vases near the mirrored elevators. I have been there only long enough to sleep. I order room service and lie to the waiter when he asks where I am from. I go downstairs and get on the bus—purple on the outside, gray on the inside. Nearly all the band and crew have gone to their bunks for a few more hours sleep. I put Bessie Smith on the stereo and think about her life. The bus we're traveling on is nicer than what she was accustomed to, I'm sure, but the essence of one-night stands and audience chemistry must be the same. Still, when Bessie played

Atlanta's old "81" theater in 1923, the mobs inside and out hung on her every note, but when I played in the same city's tony Chastain Park last night the white-wine-and-Brie crowd chatted during my entire set. Which brought up my no longer existential, but constant question: Why do I do this?

We stop at a Cracker Barrel for lunch somewhere in the Deep South. My body goes rigid and limp at the same time in defense against . . . what? The dirt-brown uniforms, the cigarette smoke, my own unpleasant memories? There is a tangible density, a sluggishness in the Deep South, born of the heat and a fiercely defended spiritual myopia. I depend on my traveling companions to smooth the hard edge of loneliness that cuts through my body, my dreams, and sometimes my performances. And I try to soothe theirs in return. I don't know how to love myself out here, and time has not been a helpful teacher in that regard.

• • •

ROSANNE CASH

Room service is a continual source of comfort. I study every new menu seriously and with great concentration and always order the same thing: pancakes, sliced banana on the side. I seldom eat more than half of it. This morning, after I push the tray away, I am seized by an overwhelming desire to talk to anyone. It's too early to phone the East Coast, practically the middle of the night on the West Coast. I call the tour manager on some flimsy pretense. He's not in his room.

A new hotel. Black curtains with a pattern of gray and beige ribbons, shirred valances, floor to ceiling. It's eleven p.m. on a day off. I go to the bar and have one drink with eight of the band and crew and laugh obligingly at all their jokes, then wish them good night. I am the first to leave, as usual.

I go back to my black-curtained room and put on headphones to listen to a string quartet. Sweet violins and cello encircle me as I lay there, but something about the curtains bothers me. I lie quietly, uneasy, but not sure why.

An image slowly surfaces, of myself, in labor with my first child. Something went wrong. There were excited nurses, hasty phone calls entreating my doctor to come to my room immediately, stretchers, footsteps, and panic. The most pernicious memory from that night has always been the curtains in the labor room, jerked open with a metal scrape and emergency flourish. I don't think I ever truly recovered from the shock and fear of that initial childbirth experience. My blessed baby was born in perfect health and with stunning beauty, but the unwarranted hysteria broke open a small chasm in my psyche from which anxiety has continued to seep for the last eleven years.

It's a familiar memory, one I have turned over in my mind hundreds of times. I let it play out, breathe deeply, and try to return to the music. The unease deepens, the curtains menace. I become agitated, and slowly, like a neon beach ball that has been released from the bottom of a pool, another tableau surfaces in my inner vision, one that makes me tear off the head-phones and cry out. My daughter, this same baby, is now two-and-a-half years old. I have taken her to a public pool for lessons in "drown-proofing." The theory presented is that if you allow a child to flounder in the water, face down, for what seems to me an interminable length of time, occasionally showing her where the air is, she will eventu-ally learn to flip herself over and float on her back. Then, if one unspeakable day she should fall into a pool with no one around, she will know what to do until someone comes to res-cue her.

The near fanaticism of the teacher plays my nerves like a steel drum. At the first lesson, my daughter sputters, thrashes in the water furiously, and resists the instructions with an admirable defiance. The teacher tells me that my child has a powerful will, which I must break in order to save her life.

I take my daughter home, close myself in my bedroom, and cry. That night, I dream that my little girl and I run from tidal wave after tidal wave, but we are unable to get out of the way of any of them in time.

The next day, the teacher has an eleven-year-old-boy demonstrate how drown-proofed he is by having him float, fully clothed, on his back for the entire lesson. My daughter again sputters, cries, resists the woman ferociously. I am afraid to trust my instincts, which are urging me to never set foot in the humid Boy's Club again, to rescue my child from the misguided instructor, and wrap her in my arms in some-place warm and safe and very dry. A misplaced sense of obligation wins out. I take her back for a third session, and this is when it happens.

We are in the water. I am ten feet from the teacher, who has taken my baby for some individual instruction. She lets her go. My daughter is face down, floundering. She hasn't yet learned how to turn herself over, and even if she had, she most likely would not give this woman the satisfaction. She continues to strug-gle. The instructor stands in the pool impas-sively. I am paralyzed. The time becomes end-less—thirty seconds, forty-five seconds. "She needs air," I insist anxiously. "No, she's okay. A child this age can stay underwater for a full two minutes," the woman says. I am watching my baby's face when suddenly, as if in slow motion, she opens her eyes wide and looks at me from underwater in confusion. I read the full message in her beautiful, plaintive brown gaze: *Why have you betrayed me? Why don't you rescue me from her?* The woman finally gives her breath back to her, as if it were a gift, instead of her natural right, and brings my daughter over to where I am standing, crying. She looks at me with contempt. "Don't come back," she says. "You can send your husband with her, but you shouldn't come back." My daughter and I are both exhausted, and we make our way silently home.

My daughter seems to forget the drown-proofing incident quickly, develops a love of the water, and soon learns to swim like a little fish. I am not getting better. My nightmares continue and worsen, and there is a sick gnawing in my stomach that alternates with the panic that seizes me in the middle of the night as I awaken from tidal wave after tidal wave. Something in me has cracked, has shattered, and I have not the slightest clue how to put it back together.

The following year, I begin seeing a hypnotist to try to lose the fifteen pounds I have carried since the birth of my second daughter a few months earlier. During the third session, as I recline in his chair, in a deeply relaxed state, and as he is planting suggestions about eating habits and weight control, an image slowly comes into focus, unbidden, before my mind's eye. I see myself, but a smaller, darker version of myself, in a house near the ocean. My older daughter is with me, but she is a few years older than I know her to be. She looks much the same. I am aware of several circumstances: that she and I are alone; that these events are taking place a very, very long time ago, and that we are both about to die.

I am angry and afraid, but resolute. I see myself take my daughter to the basement of the little house and I hear myself tell her: "When the water comes over you, take a big breath and draw it into your lungs." I look at her sternly. "You must do this." She nods. We sit against the wall in the cool, dark basement and wait. At first there is nothing but stillness, and then the roar of a million combined waves hits the house. I am holding her tightly as a torrent of seawater rushes toward us, its level rising quickly in the small space. I search her face and see her limpid brown eyes open to me with a sweet apprehensiveness. I nod to her, and she opens her mouth wide to take the salty water into her lungs. Her eyes do not close, but it is only a moment until the light in them is gone. The water enters my own lungs on the intake of a scream.

Back in the hypnotists chair, my chest feels as if it will implode. My lungs seem to weigh a hundred pounds each, and the cries that escape from them seem to have been wrested from the viscous seawater I must have carried inside me for centuries.

"Go past this," the hypnotist urges me. I am not sure what he means, but I allow my focus to pull away from the intertwined bodies floating in my inner eye, and a new picture of the two of us gradually reveals itself. We are alive and whole again, but very different from each other. She is recovered and perfect, and I am not. She smiles at me and drifts off, on to a new adventure, a new life. There is nothing left of me; no body, no plan. I am about to embark on a search for her and her forgiveness. When I find her I will never let her go.

The hour in the hypnotist's chair uncovers the hidden energy that has shaped my soul, carved my personality, and informed my dreams. I cry as if I will never stop; acrid tears from a venerable pool that has flooded the boundaries of my life.

Slowly, with his guidance, I come back to this chair, this room, this time. When I leave him, I am in a stupor and I drift for months in the memory and its afterimages.

The following summer we are at a pool party with several other families. In the midst of greetings and food being arranged on a long table, a toddler falls in at the deep end. I am the only one who sees it happen. I run to the pool, jump in, and lift the baby out. After all the adults have made a fuss, and we have seen that she is not hurt, I turn to find my daughter standing close to my side, very still, looking at me with serious, wide eyes.

"You were scared when you saw the baby's face under the water, weren't you, Mommy?"

"Yes, I was. Were you scared?"

"No," she says softly and firmly, her gaze unwavering. "I knew she would be okay."

I smile at her, reveling in everything she is and knows, and I somehow let her understand that I will be okay, too.

The road ends eight years later, in a Holiday Inn ten miles from where my children sleep in their father's house, a house I do not share. To know my children are resting so close to where I pace in a suffocatingly sterile room crystal-lizes a feeling that has been only a murmur and a sigh up until now.

Earlier, as I drove my rental car to the

hotel after leaving my children for the night, under an incandescent southern moon, I realize I have crossed a portal. I have just passed through it at ten P.M. on this October evening. The possibilities for my life, I see, are no longer endless. My options have fallen away like cracked paint on a summer house.

But the choices left to me are potent and real. Performance has become my nightly crucible and reflective pool, a place where I can take my dilemmas. My personality has found a grindstone in the presence of an audience, my fear has found a frame in which to sweat itself out. Liberation comes in two-hour doses. Under the lights I can face the inconsistencies of my soul. I can almost let go.

The moon burns and glows. My children sleep unaware. I know that they, too, will one day come to this realization: Their youth will not last, their riches will not be infinite: their faith can only be imperfect. And I am such an imperfect mother to them, no matter how many centuries I have stumbled toward absolution. I have worn my melancholy like a perfume, and they have sweltered in it, been silenced by it, gasped in its airlessness. It has been a corrosive on the bedrock of their innocence. I have struggled mightily with it in the deep rapids of self-delusions, and yet still it wafts and clings. But I have not been hardened by it. And neither will they, for even a little knowledge carries the possibility of salvation.

I face a future stripped down but anointed, if only with my own fate. I take my questions to the stage. It is surely just what I need: a balm to soothe these inner cracks, to stretch these lungs that want so badly to breathe and sing, to be bathed and purified in the light of a full southern moon that forgives my judgments of the shadows she might cast. And when the children awake—should they need me—I will stand ready to navigate all the countless and strange bodies of water they might be required to cross.

A WEEK AT THE GORE

The Gore Hotel
Queen's Gate
London SW7

To Stuart Leighton
By Facsimile

Dearest Stuart,

The girls and I arrived safely last night and made it through customs in record time. The girls' jaws hit their chests when they first saw the line of London taxis waiting outside.

Black and roomy and funny-looking, just like in the movies. They were very quiet on the ride into the city, a bit overwhelmed, I think. Our room is lovely, number 315, if you should need to contact us. (I do hope to get a note or two from you, if you're not absolutely swamped with work.) The girls are still sleeping at the moment, but after breakfast we plan to do some sightseeing and a little shopping. I will fax you tomorrow and bring you up to date on all our adventures.

Take care, darling.

With all my love,
Amanda
20 FEBRUARY 1995
10 A.M.

P.S. Don't forget to leave money for the cleaning lady. She comes tomorrow.

THE GORE HOTEL
QUEEN'S GATE
LONDON SW7

ROSANNE CASH

Dearest Stuart,

I must have lost my mind. Whatever made me think I could live in the same room with two teenagers for a week? Have you ever truly taken into consideration what two adolescent girls consume in the course of a day? It's staggering. How did I miss this at home? They seem to believe that sugar, fat, caffeine, and chocolate are the four major food groups. And is it possible that they have some kind of ocular deficiency that renders them incapable of recognizing certain everyday objects, such as wastebaskets? And, honestly, I never imagined that human beings could take such delight in performing and describing ALL their bodily functions. Plus they are such bears if they don't get their full twelve hours of sleep.

Beyond all that, we did have a good time yesterday. We walked quite a bit (only a few whines and complaints) and visited Westminster Abbey. I had forgotten how magnificent it is. The Cloisters, especially, were so serene. It was nice to walk around and ruminate on a thousand years of peaceful activity there. Unfortunately, we couldn't explore as long as I would have liked because Caroline stated emphatically that "monks creep me out." So we moved on to Covent Garden. There was a rock band playing in the courtyard, which the girls quite enjoyed. I bought a blue handknit sweater ("are you kidding, Mom?"), and the girls got a couple of things; sneakers and the like, nothing they couldn't have found in New York, but to them the most fantastic sneakers they'd ever seen. It was a tiring but exciting day.

One last thing. Jane got her period for the first time just after we arrived. If she knew I was telling you she'd kill me, but I thought you'd want to know. I think she feels very grown up, and it was cause for reflection on my part—here she stands at the cusp of womanhood (but has to be reminded to brush her teeth!). Today she asked me, "So when do I get PMS?" Well, if one has it, they all want it, I suppose.

Remember, Lydia has offered to come over and

*prepare a meal or two for you, if you'd like. Just
let her know.*

With all my love,
Amanda
21 FEBRUARY 1995
10:45 P.M.

THE GORE HOTEL
QUEEN'S GATE
LONDON SW7

TO STUART LEIGHTON
BY FACSIMILE

Dearest Stuart,

*After all these years of considering myself
fundamentally British, I find I am peculiarly
American. It is so bittersweet to visit my homeland
after so many years away, with my two teenage
daughters, who are most definitely American, and
feel slightly displaced from both cultures. Oh well, I
suppose I am both rather than neither.*

The weather couldn't be better, surprisingly enough. Great white billowy clouds and a good stiff English breeze with a biting chill to the air, which smells remarkably fresh (particularly after New York). I took the girls by the flat in Mornington Crescent I shared when I was in my early twenties. They did try to be interested and polite, but there was much scuffing of feet and pointed sighing on their parts while standing on the street in front of the building. It was a powerful moment for me, however, thinking about myself as a young girl in that miserable flat (which appears to be meticulously gentrified, from the outside, at least), never for once imagining myself as I am now. I stood there for a long moment staring at it, three floors up, trying to recapture . . . something. Or even remember. It seems like another life.

They have colored their hair; I hope you won't mind too much. They were so keen to go to a salon just off the Kensington High Street that we happened across. I left them there with a stern admonition that I would not pay for green or blue, and I went to have a stroll. I picked them up an hour and a half later. Caroline's hair is the prettiest shade of lavender, and Jane's is a bit more maroon.

ROSANNE CASH

It doesn't bother me; as Lydia always said to me
about her daughters: "If they're not doing drugs or
having sex, let them color and pierce anything they
want." Speaking of piercing, Caroline wants very
much to pierce her navel. Don't worry, I think I can
put her off for a while.

How is your project coming? Don't work
yourself to death, deadline or no deadline. I'm just
going to the lounge for a nightcap sans children. I
toast you, my love.

Always,
Amanda
22 FEBRUARY 1995
7:20 P.M.

THE GORE HOTEL
QUEEN'S GATE
LONDON SW7

TO STUART LEIGHTON
BY FACSIMILE

Dearest Stuart,
It was wonderful to hear from you, thanks so
much for the fax. The girls send hugs and kisses

back to you and say to tell you they wish you were here.

We had the definitive tourist day yesterday, beginning at Buckingham Palace, where the girls were fascinated by the guards and the size of the palace. As we walked away, I heard Jane whisper to Caroline, "I can't believe we're standing in front of Buckingham Palace." Whispers are required, you see, to not let on to me that they enjoy anything very much beyond shopping and hair coloring and eating. We then went on to Madame Tussaud's, as dreadful now as when you and I visited it. The girls were mainly interested in the Chamber of Horrors, and Caroline, who considers herself somewhat of an expert on Jack the Ripper (remember—she wrote her first freshman term paper on him) was really disappointed that more attention wasn't given him in the exhibits. "This sucks," were her exact words, I believe.

The girls have been getting on fairly well; very few quarrels, especially considering that none of us has any privacy. They are made giddy by peculiarly British habits and sayings. For instance, the young man who brought breakfast this morning set the tray down and I gave him a tip. He said "ta," as he pocketed it and left the room. I turned around to the girls to see their eyes widen, and at the same time they exclaimed, "Did he say 'ta'?" I explained that it was slang for "thanks," and they became quite hysterical. They begged me to call him back to give him another tip, but I have my limits.

They are finally in bed. Jane had trouble falling asleep, claiming that the Chamber of Horrors from Madame Tussaud's was bothering her. It just reaffirms my belief that children, no matter what their age, shouldn't be exposed to this kind of thing, but I certainly seem to be in the minority. She mustn't have been too disturbed, however, because just before she finally slept, she said, "Mom, I hope 'Ta' brings our breakfast tomorrow, don't you?"

And so now, my dear, I shall close this. I hope you aren't too lonely and that your project is going well.

With all my love,
Amanda
23 FEBRUARY 1995
11:15 P.M.

To Stuart Leighton
By Facsimile

Dearest Stuart,

I've been thinking about Mother and Dad quite a lot the last two days. I suppose I should take the train to Tunbridge Wells and visit the cemetery and see the house, but somehow I just don't have the heart for it. What do you think, Stuart? Would it be wrong of me not to go? Tomorrow is out of the question, in any case, as the girls have been reading up on the history of the Tower of London in preparation for our visit there. Of course, they mainly want to see where all the heads were whacked off.

Today we had a quiet day. Caroline wanted some privacy, so Jane and I took a long walk in Kensington Gardens and visited the palace to view the antique dress collection. We marveled over the elaborate costumes the ladies of the court used to wear. Jane was particularly struck by a turn-of-the-century heavily embroidered and beaded white gown

ROSANNE CASH

with a long train and a feathered hat. We were
struck with how small women seemed to be back
then, if the mannequins were an accurate indica-
tion. Jane could not tear herself away from a man-
nequin of a young Queen Victoria.

I'm turning in early tonight. Perhaps after
a good night's rest I'll feel able to make a decision
about the trip to Tunbridge Wells. I miss you, dar-
ling. The girls and I send all our love.

Always,

Amanda

24 FEBRUARY 1995

9:40 P.M.

THE GORE HOTEL
QUEEN'S GATE
LONDON SW7

TO STUART LEIGHTON
BY FACSIMILE

Dearest Stuart,

It's turned a bit colder today, very gray and
damp. The wind is strong; it turns umbrellas inside

out and sends newspapers hurtling across the streets. I love it, of course.

An odd thing happened with Caroline. She had an anxiety attack, or something of the sort. Last night, just when we were turning in, she began to cry and said she felt strange and frightened. She felt afraid of speaking to people, worried at being laughed at or misunderstood. She felt very alone, even with Jane and me, and insecure about who she is here in a foreign country. Of course, she didn't put it in those exact words, but that is what I gathered. She begged me to let her go home early, alone, and was very angry with me when I refused. I tried to comfort her as best I could, but she didn't want that. I think she just needed to cry it out, which she did for a few hours. It's funny, Stuart.— I expected to have all those feelings of anxiety, coming back to England, and I haven't. I've felt a sense of poignance, when I went to my old flat, and sadness contemplating a trip to Tunbridge Wells, but none of the anxiety. Caroline seems to have felt it for both of us. She is so much like me. The more she pulls away, the more I see just how similar we are.

Our visit to the Tower was a resounding success. The girls were spellbound. We spent several hours wandering around the various old buildings, seeing who was imprisoned in which tower, who was beheaded, and on which green. We ended up at the display of the crown jewels. Jane was nearly beside herself when she saw a little crown, resting on a dark velvet pillow, that Queen Victoria had commissioned for herself midway through her reign. (Jane has developed quite an obsession with her since seeing her mannequin and childhood rooms at Kensington Palace.) I heard her whisper to herself as she gazed at the crown, "Vicky rules." Caroline quietly studied all the cases of magnificent crowns, tiaras, sceptres, and assorted jewels and then turned to me and demanded, "Can you BUY this stuff?"

I haven't yet decided about the trip to Tunbridge Wells. We only have two more days, and I would like to be spontaneous with our remaining time. I'll see how I feel in the morning. I am beyond exhausted at the moment and unable to think clearly about much of anything.

Thanks so much for your second fax. Yes, it is strange that Lydia should stop by without Charles or the girls after you'd declined her invitation to dinner. Stuart, you are perhaps the last innocent man on earth. Don't worry about it. It was good

that you told her you were busy and sent her away.
I haven't a clue, either, as to what she's up to. I will
speak to her, discreetly, of course, when I return. I
am sorry to hear you're feeling lonely, but not TOO
sorry. It's gratifying to be missed.

Yours,
Amanda
25 FEBRUARY 1995
10:55 P.M.

THE GORE HOTEL
QUEEN'S GATE
LONDON SW7

TO STUART LEIGHTON
BY FACSIMILE

Dearest Stuart,

What a very long day I have had. I awoke
early and knew at once that I wanted to go to
Tunbridge Wells. The girls and I had a quick break-
fast and got to the train. Very little moaning on
their part, surprisingly. I think they were curious to

ROSANNE CASH

see where their old mum had been brought up and where their grandparents are buried.

Nothing is as I remember it, Stuart. Do you find that strange? I was bemused and felt somewhat detached, as if I were visiting a place I had seen in a film. The house is unchanged, physically, but seems smaller (don't people always say that?). What is completely different is its . . . personality, I guess. It has a different air. It was not forbidding. It was as if the energy had been drained out of it, and it was just a shell. I suppose that is exactly what has happened. It isn't filled with tears and shouts and suffering anymore. Or perhaps it is; I don't know who lives there now. But at least they are not my tears and suffering.

We went to the cemetery, were the girls saw their grandparents' graves for the first time. It's been well kept up, I was pleased to see.

I'm trying to think what I should say to you about it. I'm trying to think how I felt, but, honestly there were no grand epiphanies, no tortured regrets, just a sense of calm and acceptance. Jane and Caroline asked questions that I was finally ready to answer, and I was able to see myself in a clear light through their eyes. I was born to mother those girls. It has been the redemption of my life. I would most likely have self-destructed in that awful flat in Mornington Crescent had I not been led into motherhood by you.

As we left the cemetery, the girls were walking away and I turned to follow them. I glanced up, and just for a moment, with the sunlight in front of her half-blinding me, Caroline's strong back and shoulders looked just like my father's. I thought of him walking across the field, as he used to, head bent, not speaking to anyone, and we children following, afraid to speak to him. He was a different man in the fields, in the late afternoon, than he was in the evenings when he was drinking. Staring at the muscled curve of my sweet daughter's back, I missed him, for a moment, for the first time in twenty-four years. Maybe it wasn't even him I missed, but just an idea of what he might have been like with love and an education. Oddly, it was a relief to long for him, even briefly. Well, I suppose that is a small epiphany of sorts, and really all that I need or want. I wasn't looking for a great purge of emotion, or a resolution of my past. It was enough.

We came back to the Gore and had a quiet

dinner, and I splurged on chocolate cake with the girls, at their insistence. They are now engrossed in a soap opera of some kind and I am lying here thinking of you and wondering how your *week has been. I can't wait to hear it all, to deliver these children to you for a short reprieve, and to curl up next to you and fall asleep. I'm glad I'm not young, Stuart. I do so love this little path we have carved in the world.*

Our flight information is written on the calendar in the kitchen, on tomorrow's date. Don't come too early, or you'll have to wait too long. Just give us a little time to clear customs, and we'll meet you outside.

Until tomorrow.

With all my love,
Amanda
26 FEBRUARY 1995
11:35 P.M.

help in six languages

Elsa was winding slowly through the crowds down the narrow street on a cool summer evening when she heard a gunshot. She jumped and hastily smoothed the front of her white linen shirt and kept walking. When she turned the corner onto Rue Alnoye, she saw all eyes in the bistro across the street staring in one direction. She followed their gaze to see a man lying in front of a bar, with another man standing on his chest. She stopped, horrified, and instantly the man on the ground jumped up, laughing, and the two ran into the bar, where all the patrons applauded them and broke into a song.

"Morons," she muttered to herself.

The next day, she took the train to Paris, as she had planned. It was a small moment, quite insignificant, the evening before, but it stuck with her, as most unpleasant surprises did. She knew how to call for help in six languages and she rehearsed them all as she sat looking out the window at Belgian cows and green ponds, hay bales and open fields.

There was no sign welcoming her to France, so at about eleven o'clock she just assumed she had crossed the border. Purple meadows and a glimpse of a village cemetery were followed by a bright and very tidy field of mustard. She ran her fingers through her recently cut short black hair. Surely this must be France.

She was alone, with a heavy bag, for she couldn't bear to be without all her favorite shoes. "Très lourd," she grew used to saying to taxi drivers and hotel bellmen. She dragged the bag on its wheels, which were rather useless, through the length of the train station in

Paris, and bumped and clattered down two flights of stairs, while a small group waited at the bottom for her to pass.

It was the summer that would begin the second half of her life; she had seen it coming as early as a year ago. There was nothing to do but get away from all things familiar, and look at a lot of art while she was giving birth to her middle-aged self. And take along a lot of choices in footwear, given the unpredictability of the new path.

The evening before, just before she had come upon the fake murder scene, she had stopped in the Grand Plaza, which was ringed by ancient and elaborate mansions. On the far side of the plaza, she noticed about forty police officers, in full riot gear. *Perhaps they come out every evening, as a safety measure*, she thought uneasily. But shortly, a rowdy parade of young people marched into the square, shouting in unison, something about French involvement in Rwanda. Or maybe about World Cup soccer. It was impossible for her to translate the slang colored with so much anger. Elsa stood at the corner of the plaza, ready to bolt if necessary. She ran her eyes around the square at the glorious houses, sculpted and luxuriously scalloped, verandaed and towered, spectacular in the sheen of late afternoon light, and kept one eye on the crowd. This square must have seen many such protests and riots, not to mention a fair number of beheadings and hangings. It was nothing new. Frustrated young voices bounced off four-hundred-year-old walls. Violent impulses were gently disarmed by the long-suffering gargoyles and regal female heads that were carved into the stone above the doorways. Enter, but beware. We are always watching. The protestors soon turned silly, and by the time she left they were dancing and kissing.

roses and bells

In Paris, in her single bed, in her tiny room that overlooked a courtyard, Elsa lay and listened to the voices rising from the café, thinking of her children, a boy and a girl, and of the myriad ways in which she had failed them. These were the arrows that stayed permanently embedded in her heart, and on sleepless nights, when she was far away from them, an unseen hand twisted the shafts. The air in the courtyard was very still and warm, and smelled faintly of cooking and geraniums. She had been a loving mother, but preoccupied. Worse, she had been moody and capricious, and her children had had to digest these indulgences on a daily basis. The magnitude of the various ways she might have undermined their innocence and freedom had gathered weight in her conscience over the years until it reached a palpable density. One by one, memories of her shortcomings, great and small, surfaced in her awareness, expanded, and filled her body, her thoughts, and her solitude, which might have been so luminous, with lead. Her high school English students, not her own children, had received the best, the most stable and inspired parts of herself. That realization was what had compelled her to quit teaching. She had made it up to her children, she was sure. She had gotten much better in the last few years. They were nearly grown, and as far as she could tell, had turned out to be fine people, but she could not stop making herself pay.

A vase of roses in the room filled the space around her head with their intense, single-note scent. She had bought them that afternoon at the street market. She could not see them in the darkness, but she was keenly aware of them, five feet away on the slightly battered, child-sized brown desk. She envisioned them carefully: white petals, edged in a velvety deep pink, which bled sweetly into a paler pink, a dozen of them, some starting to open, some tight buds still, a profusion of fat, oily green leaves, and that was it. In her mind, she examined them from every perspective, until she drifted off. In the night, she awoke to the familiar heaviness in her chest, the numbness in her legs she had not absolved with the roses, and realized she'd have to find another remedy. There would be bells in the morning, she remembered. Lots of bells, ringing from all the churches nearby. There would be bells in the morning, and she imagined their bronze peals and sincere echoes until the weight lifted and she fell asleep

ROSANNE CASH

again, and it was not long until their raucous
reality awakened her.

st-julien-le-pauvre

There was a man she had seen the day before.
After she arrived in Paris, she had walked to
Notre Dame, dutifully marveling at its magnif-
icence, yet unable to talk herself into any real
passion for its cold grandeur. She wanted to
feel the force of the accumulated residue of
seven hundred years of prayers. She wanted
her bones to vibrate with the magnetic reso-
nance of the saints. Maybe the millions of people who came every year to gawk and snap
photos, herself included, had just drained the
sacredness from it. She left, and walked across
the bridge to the little church of St-Julien-le-
Pauvre. As Elsa stepped into the cool darkness,
she inhaled deeply with pleasure. It was so
lovely, so delicate and old, she could hardly
bear it. She took a seat close to the front, to
study the ancient carvings and tapestries and
the stones bearing the names of the martyrs
who rested in the walls. Elsa thought of her

ex-husband, somewhat of an expert in ancient architecture, and how much he would love this place. She realized then that he had most certainly been here, when he was in graduate school, cataloguing and studying the cathedrals and abbeys of Europe. While they were married, they had visited many of them together. He had always felt compelled, upon entering a grand edifice, to launch into a somewhat pedantic discourse on the history of that particular house of God, delivered in a breathy monotone, more to himself than her. She could not remember being in silence in a church in her entire adult life. But now, she was alone in the way she loved most: with a minimum of rational thought, childish impulses and needs unexpectedly disarmed, vague but stirring memories drifting in and out. She felt herself truly occupy her body and settle into its far corners and deep curves. *This is mine*, she thought. *This is a place that has always waited for me. I know this room and this space, and it belongs to me. There is no boundary between me and it.* When she felt it to be entirely real, she got up to leave.

ROSANNE CASH

Just outside the door, with the afternoon light hitting his profile full on and making him seem incandescent in the shadow of the entrance, stood an old man with an upside-down gray felt hat outstretched in his hand. He did not nod or say a word, but looked directly in her eyes, a breath of a cautious smile on his lips. His skin was the color of butter in this light, with an oily sheen like the leaves of her roses. He was small, and as perfectly formed as an origami ornament, or the Pietà come to life. She wanted to touch him, but instead just nodded and dropped a few francs into his hat. She stepped fully into the sunlight and slowly began making her way toward St Séverin. When she turned around, he was gone.

Now, as she listened to the bells, she wondered about him. Perhaps he was as old as St-Julien-le-Pauvre. Maybe he had been standing there, hand outstretched, since the twelfth century. Maybe only the style of the hat had changed. Maybe he knew her, and she knew him. Perhaps someone from another life had come to visit.

She was happy suddenly. It was all she needed really. The church, her body, the bells, roses slowly opening, Maria Callas echoing through the courtyard from an unseen stereo, and a perfect old man who waits, as calmly and patiently as St. Julien himself, in the cool shadows of the centuries, and asks for what he wants without saying a word.

the girl and the flute

She went back to St-Julien-le-Pauvre that evening for a concert of Handel and Mozart on an unaccompanied flute. The interior smelled faintly of a crypt. She hadn't noticed it before, the centuries of damp and stale air hanging like a comforting incense. She found a seat near the front of the church and applauded politely when the flutist walked out and bowed. Elsa read in the program that she was twenty-six years old. She was a lovely girl, pale and a bit fragile-looking. She began to play, and her flute echoed among the vaulted ceilings and off the thick stone walls. She frowned anxiously as she worked her way through each piece, eyes widening and her cheeks turning a deep pink with every long note she sustained. The church was so quiet you could hear every urgent intake of her breath. She looked as if she might faint at any moment, and though Elsa could not bear to look at her, neither could she turn away. The girl was wearing a black linen summer dress, with a halter top and a modest split in the skirt, so that as she sat in the straight wooden chair her leg was revealed to just above the knee. Her chest and neck were unlined. Elsa squinted her eyes to preview the damage the years would do to her flawless skin. The music of the young and unaware, played to perfection, was filling the air around the remains of the holy who rested in the walls of St-Julien-le-Pauvre. The musician's tender, unlined skin stretched over bones no different than those of the saints crumbling a few feet away. Elsa squeezed her eyes shut tightly, to shut out the relentlessness of time. At a break in the program, she left, but no little man waited outside the church.

the cigarette butt

For two days in a row she had found a cigarette butt on the floor next to her bed, though she herself didn't smoke. She called the woman at the reception desk, an animated, long-suffering, dark Frenchwoman who had already graciously dealt with her complaints of smelly drains and noisy pipes, and told her of her discovery.

"*Merde*," Elsa heard her say, under her breath and away from the phone. "Is not possible," she declared loudly.

"But it is possible. I'm looking at the butt right now. This is the second day a butt has been here," Elsa said, shifting her weight from one sandaled foot to the other.

"Perhaps the man who comes to look at the drain who smells left it in your room, Madame," she announced firmly.

"No, Madame," Elsa replied, equally firm. "I was in the room when he came to smell the drain." She scratched at a spot on her blue jeans. There was no hurry.

"Perhaps it is the same cigarette from yesterday." The woman was unmovable.

ROSANNE CASH

"No, no, Madame. I threw yesterday's butt away yesterday," Elsa replied, waiting expectantly.

"Madame," the Frenchwoman declared, "this house is very safe. You are not to worry."

Elsa squirmed. She hated it when people told her not to worry. Worry was a very private affair, on a par with sex and religion. But she decided to accommodate her.

"Yes," she said slowly but agreeably, "perhaps the wind blew it in my window. Two days in a row. That's it, I'm sure. It's okay, yes, really, thank you very much, *merci beaucoup*." As Elsa hung up, she bent over and picked up the stubborn little butt and threw it in the wastebasket. She stood for a moment, hands on hips, staring out at the courtyard.

Ten minutes later, Madame and the manager of the hotel, proper in a little bow tie, knocked on her door. Elsa opened it, and they marched in and inspected the spot on the floor where the cigarette butt had lain.

"Is not possible." Madame straightened. "No one could come into your room, Madame. Perhaps someone sees you from across the courtyard, and throws it at you." Madame smiled provocatively.

Elsa flushed and looked out the window. The possibility had crossed her mind, but it was at least fifty feet across the courtyard.

"He'd have to have a pretty good arm," Elsa said, more to herself than to the pair. She nodded at both of them. "It's okay, really. I'm sure the wind blew it in. Twice. Two days in a row, actually, but it's possible. Same time of day, same place next to the bed. It's definitely possible." She shrugged. "And you say no one could get in my room."

Madame and the owner, who had not said a word, stiffened formally. "No, Madame. Not possible. We have the only key."

"All right then," Elsa nodded. She pulled on a few strands of hair at the back of her neck.

As the pair moved toward the door, Madame stopped at the bathroom, sticking her head in and sniffing loudly.

"Oh, your man fixed it. It's much better!" Elsa said vigorously, sniffing in response and smiling. "It's just perfect! Whatever he did cleared up the smell instantly."

ROSANNE CASH

"Ah ha!" Madame and the owner both drew themselves up with pride and walked confidently to the door.

"Thank you for coming up," Elsa said, closing the door behind them. She went to the window and, in the dimming light, searched the windows across the courtyard for a strong arm attached to a mean spirit. Seeing nothing, she pulled the curtain closed.

the butcher cries

The wind came up out of nowhere, the temperature dropped ten degrees, and that night she had a dream. She dreamt of her butcher back home. She had seen this man nearly every week, for years, as he chopped her chicken into parts and hand-rolled her sausages. His left hand was thumbless. It had taken her nearly three years to ask him about it.

"Virgil, how did you lose your thumb?"

The butcher stopped what he was doing and looked up at her. His wide eyes instantly filled with tears, which gathered and fell over his bottom lids in huge, clear drops, the tears of a man who had saved them for a truthful moment. They rolled down his face and off his chin, splashing soundlessly into the bloody meat he was holding. Elsa took a shocked step backwards.

"It was the day my daughter died. I had to come to work. I was chopping, I wasn't thinking, you know . . . " He shrugged. He sighed and wiped his face with both red-stained sleeves and went back to his work, shaking his head.

In the dream, he was walking with her across a moat, over a field, and away from a castle. It was near sundown, and the worn stones of the castle and the field of yellow knee-high grass were shining in the warm late afternoon light. He was wearing his blood-stained white butcher's uniform, carrying his cleaver, and talking slowly and carefully to Elsa.

He never looked back at the castle, though it was heartbreakingly beautiful in the golden light. Elsa was tripping over her own feet because she could not stop craning her head back over her shoulder, could not take her eyes off it.

"Nothing stays the same, Elsa. Nothing. Not your children, not your work, not your life. The harder you try to make it stay the same, the worse it's going to hurt when it changes." He paused, blinking hard, waiting for more words, as if he were reading them from an invisible page held just in front of him. "Everything worth having requires a sacrifice, that's true. And then once you get it, it changes. And then you change. Nothing you can do about that." He nodded slightly.

Elsa was only half-listening. She squinted her eyes back at the castle, to see how it might have looked before the years had done their damage, when the stones had been smooth and whole. It was so clear. It had been someone's home, surely. Lives had been lived there. It had housed a family. It had outlived its usefulness.

They had walked far across the field, to a lone tree at its edge.

"Very few things worth hanging onto, anyway," the butcher said with a faint smile. "And not much at all worth rotting your insides over."

He stopped at the tree and, raising his right hand, rested it on the trunk, spreading his thumb apart from his fingers. He lifted the cleaver with his left hand high over his head. She stared at him, horrified, but could not move. He turned to look at her, and tears filled his big eyes, spilling over his bottom lids and falling down his cheeks.

"You were never a bad mother," he said, and brought the cleaver down.

She woke up suddenly, heart racing.

"No," she said aloud. She got up, shaking and stiff, and went to the bathroom and turned on the light. Her thighs felt sticky. She looked down to see blood dripping onto the blue tiled floor. She had gotten her period in her sleep. She cleaned herself up and crawled back into bed, all tremors and pounding temples, and within seconds, was sound asleep. No smell of roses, no sound of bells, only her own blood for absolution: into the deep sleep of the blameless, caressed by dreams and old lives.

. . .

Near the Panthéon, at the church of St-Etienne-du-Mont, was the shrine of Ste. Geneviève. Elsa went there on her last day in Paris, wandering into it accidentally after a tedious and depressing visit to the Panthéon. The great and ugly necropolis of the Panthéon, in which the bodies of Voltaire, Rousseau, and other rational icons rested, was host to tours and scores of camera toting visitors, and was given several pages in the guidebooks, while the tomb of Ste. Geneviève lay unobtrusive, and for the most part unnoticed, not fifty yards away. Inside the church was a little chapel in honor of the patron saint of Paris. Her body had been cruelly disposed of during the Revolution, but the sarcophagus and earth from her tomb were carefully protected under gold latticework.

A woman was standing at the tomb, hands resting on the gold grille, eyes closed, lips moving silently in prayer. She was about fifty, conservatively dressed in a print skirt and ivory cotton blouse with pearl buttons. She wore good brown leather walking shoes and carried a small handbag in the crook of her arm. Her hair was neatly pulled back with a lapis clip.

Elsa circled her and the tomb at a respectful distance, watching closely, waiting. She stopped at a small altar nearby, her back to a cluster of thin novena candles, most of them alight with small white flames. The woman kept praying. Elsa glanced over at the wide rows of pews and saw a girl sitting and staring quietly at the great altar at the front of the church. One row behind her, a young man played with her long hair, running it through his fingers, tugging gently, occasionally whispering something into her ear. The girl paid him no attention, her eyes never leaving the altar. Elsa looked back at the praying woman. Her lips had stopped moving, and she stood silently, head bowed, eyes closed, hands now folded in prayer. She reached out and lightly touched the grille once more, then turned, nodded politely to Elsa, and walked away.

Elsa approached the tomb. She rubbed her damp palms on her jeans and glanced around self-conciously. What prayer did one offer at the birth of middle age? Perhaps such a gesture wasn't essential, but here she was. It couldn't hurt. She laid her hands tentatively on the grille, and instantly withdrew them. It was giving off heat, or a vibration, she couldn't tell which. She felt a little dizzy and confused, and looked over at the pews. Empty. The girl and boy were gone. Elsa's forehead was damp, and her hair was curling with moisture on her neck. She was suddenly very hungry, more hungry than she could remember being since she was a child. She glanced back at the enormous front door of the church and was startled to see there, standing in the pink light pouring in through the stained glass windows on either side of the entrance, the old man from St-Julien-le-Pauvre. His hat was in his hand, grasped lightly and held away from his body, its brim pointing to the ground. He was staring at her. When he caught her eye, he smiled shakily but widely, drew up his little bones to their full height, and with a barely perceptible tremble, doffed his hat to her and walked slowly out of the church. The heavy wooden door closed behind him with a solid thud.

Elsa turned back to the lattice work, shaking slightly, and her tears fell through the grille, onto the uncommon tomb of Ste. Geneviève (surely not the first tears to dampen the patron's resting place), and she could almost hear a little hiss and see a whisper of smoke as the drops hit the stones.

What prayer did one offer up when one had more questions than requests? What held her in this body? Her love of art, her appreciation of small kindnesses, her ability to be truly happy for the success of others? Her worry, her jealousy, her scars? Was there enough innocence left in her for supplication? Was there enough self-forgiveness in her to approach the saint with an open heart?

She placed her hands gingerly on the gold lattice. Words came to her, not a prayer but a declaration, inspired by living a life that felt so much longer than it actually was. Into the empty tomb, she said,

"I am a woman,
which is to say,
part girl and part suffering.

ROSANNE CASH

The first half of my life
has been utterly absorbed
by other people
and by my own demons.
The second half
I will spend laughing."

SHELLY'S VOICES

the priestess

I have always heard voices. I have always answered them, in whispers and sighs: the cruel ones, the petulant ones, the sinister ones, and the small, resonant one at the center of my being that tells the others to fuck off, when I remember to ask her to. I do not court insanity, but I flirt outrageously. As of late, the flirtation has taken on a strident tone. Yesterday, peering into my closet, I heard myself scream out loud, "I will not tolerate it any longer!" The sheer volume took me across an inner but absolute boundary. Yet it dawns on me that true insanity is not the thing I fear most, although most of my voices seem to believe it is, but rather the tunnel of obsession through which I must crawl on my way to madness that really horrifies me. In that tunnel, my very bones become prison bars. Food, work, sex, sleep, and pain become fun-house mirrors, and I gape and wrestle with the distorted images of myself they reflect.

I surface ten, twenty times a day, always with a rush of pins and needles that begins in my solar plexus and spreads quickly through my entire body. And always with the same thought: *Where was I and how long was I gone?* I had descended into the vertebrae of my neck. I was walking across a lighted bridge that careened into my view from twenty thousand feet in the air. I was watching the life drain from my body via the slashes in my wrists, watching the blood darken the pale wood of the floor of a one-room flat in Prague in the last century, in another life. I feel there is more than one person who thinks my thoughts.

ROSANNE CASH

. . .

I wake from a deep sleep at four A.M. I am lying on my stomach. I lift my head suddenly and stare at the wall, which is inches from my face. "What is it?" I demand angrily. A bluish image comes into focus. I see myself, fourteen years old, dead at the bottom of a swimming pool. Exasperated, I conjure up an image of an angel in a blue velvet dress to pull my adolescent self from the bottom of the pool and out into the stars of the galaxy, where the girl who was me becomes alive again as she soars through the interstellar dust, holding the hand of the winged one, and more alive the farther they fly. I close my eyes in relief, turn over, and go back to sleep.

When I think I am alone, a staggering range of events can occur. Televisions and lamps turn themselves on and off, doorbells ring incessantly, my answering machine talks to me when it notices I have walked into the room, mirrors fall, and smells and sounds waft to me from an unseen world. These things and more: prophetic visions and dreams, time travel, and telepathy are my everyday afflictions. I tell no one. I know what is acceptable. I confided a few of the more blatant disturbances to a close friend once, and he sent me a pouch of herbs and charms from a voodoo shop, guaranteed to rid my house of ghosts. If it were only as simple as ghosts.

The world is my asylum. I am called upon daily to perform miracles and absolutions. I am the priestess and the committee, the prison and the garden, and the patients are all me.

the deity

The Deity is a five-year-old girl with enormous dark eyes and a strangely mature demeanor. Her capacity for pain is infinite— it is what makes her Divine. The Deity sleeps on a twin bed beneath a mural of Alice in Wonderland. She is silent, and her Silence harkens to what we were like before intelligence and inspiration drained away and insanity took hold like a parasite. The Deity is fragile, almost invisible; not many can really see her. She is ignored, reviled, trivialized, dismissed, reprimanded, misunderstood, punished, and severed from the sort of contact she needs most. She is beaten and screamed at, she is provoked to tears, but still she says nothing. She would like to remind us that her capacity for pain is infinite; have we stopped to consider this? Eventually, she is pushed past the point of tears. Other children cry, wail, scream, protest, sob, and complain. But her Silence is as remarkable as the Marianas trench, the very depths of the ocean. An experiment that fails, the Deity succumbs. Her perfect intelligence fails her, she becomes like the rest of us, and madness worms its way in. We had such high hopes. We were far too optimistic, in the face of such onslaughts. The Deity is a five-year-old girl. She exists out of time. It is my lot in life, my honor and command, to remember her.

• • •

I am leaning against a wall at Concourse B at O'Hare, drinking a Coke. A little girl is dragged past me by her father, who berates her and pulls her faster than she can walk and finally spanks her, once, but so hard that she is lifted a foot off the ground. She slowly turns tear-filled eyes to me—to me, as if she knew I was standing there, and locks her gaze on my face for three seconds. There is no possible chance she will escape from this man. The agony on that tiny face is inconceivable. I want to hurt him, I want to knock him down, I want to slam my fist into his face, I want to draw blood, I want to steal his child and tell her that none of this is her fault. Her face haunts me for years. For years, I remember the look on that baby's face. The Deity is a five-year-old girl. Her capacity for pain is infinite.

I visit a rehabilitation center for crack addicts and their children. I go to the in-house nursery school, where the toddlers have their toys and books, and I meet a little girl, about two years old, who is disconsolate and crying for all she is worth. She wanders around the room, wailing and distracted. Her mother, a large, sulky woman, makes half-hearted attempts to soothe the child, but she does not seem to be able to focus her attention on what is going on for more than a few seconds. The child is so disturbed, so completely disconnected, that her spirit seems to circle a few feet above her dark and driven little body. I make awkward and painful little cooing sounds because I am hoping that if she will let me connect with her for just a moment, perhaps I can explain to her, without words, which would only add to the cacophony inside her, that it is not her fault that she was pumped full of fire and poison before she even had a chance to draw her first breath. I understand fully that she doesn't begin to know how to stay inside her own body when her nervous system is detonating. Knowledge drains away, insanity sets in, the Deity succumbs before my eyes. I send the center clothing, stuffed animals, coloring books and crayons. Maybe if she finds the courage to embody herself, she might want to draw something, or confide to a stuffed bear.

Maybe the sparkly blue shoes will be a pleasant distraction for a few seconds from the utter disarray of her life. Maybe I should just give up; crayons and shoes will not heal, will not even touch, a mortally wounded soul.

I have a dream. In this dream I go to visit my child, who I have forgotten exists. She is imprisoned in a glass cell. The only thing in the cell with her is a red tricycle. She is barely big enough to ride it, but that is what she does, day after day, tracing circles around her glass cell. There is a guard, a mean and dried-up woman, who says to my child over the intercom, in the most official and impersonal way, "Shelly, you have a visitor. Your mother is here to see you." I interrupt, "Shelly, mama's here," and on the monitor next to the intercom I see her pale baby face light up like pearls in sunlight. She is not angry that I have left her and forgotten her; she is not even resentful. She is overjoyed that I have come. In my dream, my chest cracks open inside like a ripe watermelon. I wake up, and in my half-asleep state I go over the scene several times. I cannot fall back asleep. I decide to play out the dream a little further. In my mind I walk up to the mean guard and I say, "Fuck you, I'm taking her." I am steeled for a confrontation. To my astonishment, the guard shrugs casually, and before she turns to wander off, she says, "She was yours all along."

The Deity is a five-year-old girl, and all ages below that and some above. The Deity is an ongoing experiment. She awaits reclaiming. She needs peace and quiet, and a little time to reflect. She needs to be granted the authority to set the pace for awhile. Her capacity for pain, infinite as it is, is exceeded only by her capacity for joy, given a little time to heal. We have such high hopes. It is my lot in life, my honor and command, to hope.

where home is

Into the crumbling whiteness of dreams she wanders. Through the hospitals and houses, the marbled foyers and freight elevators, the lone cottage and graveled beach, she wanders. In the ancient villages and tall skyscrapers, across blackened seas and glacial rust, through the past and into the future, she wanders.

It is where she lives. There are no dreams she will not have. She would prefer anything other than the underwater ones, but even those she does not begrudge. She appears in all her guises: sister, lover, friend, the old man with four eyes who rides the elevator, the baby with the ancient face, the goddess at the funeral pyre (Oh, how she shone in that setting), the woman with cancer who sells antiques. In Shelly's frequent appearances she has a great deal to say, and requires perfect silence in which to say it. She doesn't fear the Voices; she silences them with a glance. Logic doesn't concern her, nor does it give her a moment's pause. She will hope for anything, given an opportunity.

There are reasons I know so much about her. There is justification for me to be the translator of her messages.

I suspect she is me.

ROSANNE CASH

She is the prison and the garden, the priestess and the child.

Into the crumbling whiteness, hand in hand, we wander.

DINNER

Kevin and I were the first to arrive at the restaurant, a tiny, closely packed French place with beamed ceilings and an open oven, almost hidden in the Village on West Fourth Street. We sat silently, avoiding each other's eyes, the aftermath of an argument hanging between us, and ordered a bottle of wine in advance of our dinner companions, who were invariably late.

Kevin and I had been living together for five years, having met a year earlier at a weekend art workshop

which I had taught. He liked women in authority, no matter how feeble or contrived the position. He had never told me that directly, but I
knew it was part of his early infatuation, and
his later resentment. In truth, any authority I
might have had over him did not extend
beyond that weekend, but he remained fixated
on those original assigned roles, and explored
them in a thousand subtle ways, and I was per-
versely loath to clue him in that it was a dance
he was doing alone.

I was relieved when Alex and Jean finally
appeared at the door, vibrating from the cold
air and their hurrying. They quickly came to
the table, laughing and chattering.

"My God, it takes longer to get from our
apartment down here than it does to get to
Newark, for chrissakes," Jean complained
good-naturedly.

"Oh, come on. Isn't it a thrill for you to
venture below Fourteenth Street?" I said, smiling only slightly. I wasn't crazy about Jean. "See
how the other half lives?"

Alex and Kevin exchanged a sideways hug
as Alex removed his coat and sat down. They

had known each other since boyhood and had long since lost any self-conciousness in the way they related. Alex and Jean settled themselves, and Kevin poured wine all around. There was a sudden silence, not uncomfortable but unexpected. Alex smiled at each of us in turn, in that peculiar way he behaved as if he always had a secret he wasn't sharing.

"I remember dinner conversations almost verbatim, you know. Sometimes I go home and write them down," Alex said mysteriously, rolling up the sleeves of his blue oxford shirt. Alex was bulky, not unattractively so, and hairy, not excessively so, but the combination of the two made me a little queasy, and I avoided looking at his thick, bare forearms. I couldn't help but imagine those beefy wrists and hands with a lot of gold jewelry on them, and I shuddered a little.

"You do not. Do you? That's very interesting," I said, a little nervously.

"He does," said Jean. "It's scary." She tossed her head a little. "Why do you do that, Alex? I've forgotten." She twirled one of her large pearl earrings with her fingers.

Alex looked at her, annoyed, and didn't answer. Kevin, who had been looking for a waiter, turned back to the table, distracted until this fleeting moment of tension. He lifted his eyebrows cautiously.

"What?" he said, looking at me, almost accusingly.

"Alex was just saying that he has a photographic memory for dinner conversation, so be careful what you say," I explained. I was squirming in my chair.

"What a waste of neurons, Alex," Kevin said drily. He smoothed his dark blond hair back with both hands. He was so gorgeous, but half the time I wished he were a woman so I could really talk to him. When I felt desperate, I hated him. It was also true that I adored him.

"Did we order?" he asked me blankly, knowing we had not.

"Only wine," I reminded him, and Jean and I picked up our glasses at the same time and took long drinks. As my heavy silver bracelets clanged against the crystal, I saw Jean look at my arm out of the corner of her eye. She wasn't crazy about me, either.

"Did you see Mark when he was in the city?" Kevin asked Alex.

"Mark L? No, was he in town? He moved to the Midwest, didn't he? Indiana, I think."

"Illinois, actually, Al, but you're close. It does start with an I." They both laughed.

"Who is Mark L?" I asked indifferently. I was not in the mood for Kevin's litany of old friends and where they were now.

"A guy we knew in high school. He was a year ahead of us, wasn't he, Al? Or was it two? We hung out a lot up until he got married. I ran into him last week."

I finally caught the waiter's eye and smiled expectantly.

"Would you like to order?" he asked as he glided to the table and took out his pad.

"Go ahead, Jean," Alex said, not lifting his eyes from the menu.

I waited until last, taking my time to study the menu, and carefully ordered sea bass and mushrooms in passable French, and smiled at the waiter sweetly, almost conspiratorially.

"*Merci*." The waiter disappeared.

"Aren't you sick of waiters from Queens with fake French accents?" Jean said softly, and rolled her eyes.

I ignored her. "Oh, I forgot to tell you what happened to me today." I searched Kevin's face, looking for an opening.

"What?" Kevin glanced at me impatiently.

"I was walking across Twelfth Street at about eleven o'clock, and this red-haired man came walking toward me, bleeding from his head and holding a bloody handkerchief."

"Ugh!" Jean turned her head away.

I payed no attention to Jean and kept talking. "And he said 'Ma'am, can you help me?' At first I didn't answer because I was scared, but then he seemed like he wasn't crazy, you know, just a normal guy, kind of pathetic, actually, so I said, 'What happened to you?'" I glanced around the table. Alex was looking at me politely, Jean was turned slightly away, and Kevin was studying his water glass. I warmed to my story.

"So he said that two guys on Second Avenue had jumped him and beat him up. I took a dollar out of my pocket and handed it to him while he was telling me this. He looked so sad. He was a tourist, probably. I think he had a southern accent. He asked me where the nearest subway station was that would get him back to Port Authority, and I told him, but he seemed so distraught, he wasn't really taking it in. So I said, 'Do you understand? Go one block over to Sixth Avenue and turn right and go two blocks to Fourteenth Street.' And he just kept looking sad and he handed me back the dollar and said, 'I have money, ma'am.' And he walked off, like he was broken-hearted. I felt bad. I think all he wanted was for me to walk him to the subway station. All day I was thinking about him and that bloody handkerchief. It was, well, it was shocking."

Kevin reached for the wine bottle and began refilling the glasses. I was trembling a little, with the memory of the incident. I took a breath.

"Yeah, there are a hundred stories a day like that in New York," Alex said uninterestedly, shaking his head.

"Agnes, that's entirely too long a conversation to have on the street with a perfect stranger," Kevin said testily. "It's dangerous. You shouldn't even have stopped walking."

"He wasn't perfect. He was bleeding." I said, and took another long drink of red wine.

The waiter appeared with the appetizers, and we all gazed at one another's plates.

"Oh, yes, I forgot, your mother called while you were out doing your errands today. Twice." I announced defiantly, looking Kevin directly in the eyes. He gave me a look back that said *you are so pathetic*, and his mouth hardened. He was right. It gave me no pleasure to annoy him, but I could not help myself. My options with him were so limited, I would take whatever effect I could get. After a moment he picked up his fork. Jean looked at me carefully, and I could feel her eyes travel quickly down my body before they returned to her plate. I was dressed discreetly, but elegantly, in a long black skirt and sweater. I wore no make-up, and the silver bracelets were my only jewelry. Jean finds me too austere, too dark and monastic.

I could practically hear her thoughts. Jean herself prefers a more glamorous look and is not afraid of bright colors and fun jewelry. I dress myself out of fear, and I knew she knew it.

"Mmmm, delicious," I said, biting into a mushroom. I could see Jean looking at me again out of the corner of her eye. I knew she considered it a sign of ill-breeding to praise less than extraordinary food, but, thankfully, I didn't *eat* out of fear. This was an arena where I showed impressive confidence. She sniffed.

"How is your work coming, Kev?" Alex asked.

"All right, I suppose. I just walked off a job, though. Luckily I got more work the next day."

"Why'd you walk?"

"The director was the queen bitch from hell." Kevin glanced at me to gauge my reaction. I gave him none. "She hired me as her art director, then told me I couldn't tell red from blue. She was abusive and condescending basically, so I quit."

"Good for you!" Jean's eyes glowed. "Why should you stay and be mistreated?"

It was my turn to sniff in Jean's direction. People who didn't know the whole story should withhold their opinions.

"Exactly what I thought," Kevin said. I could feel him throw another look at me, but I kept my attention focused on my appetizer.

"What's going on with you, Jean?" I asked politely, cutting precisely into another mushroom.

"Oh, very busy. I'm doing direct mail for a new bridal magazine, fundraising for a community garden on the Upper East Side, lots of exciting stuff." She lifted her head and smiled down at me. "And you?"

"I have three classes I'm teaching this semester," I answered. "Two painting classes and a drawing class. So, I'm busy, too. I'm enjoying it a lot." I smiled, genuinely, at Jean but she had turned to her food. "It's remarkable, what I learn from these eighteen- and nineteen-year- old kids I teach," I said, twirling my silver bracelets. "They think they have so many choices. Not just in art, but in their whole lives." There was silent eating around the table. "And they do, don't they? They have all the possibilities in the world, and all the time in the world. It's frightening, I think, to be faced with so much freedom every day." Alex and Jean looked at me as if I were speaking Chinese. Kevin distractedly pulled apart a sourdough roll. "I do learn a lot, I must say. I'm glad someone out there is nineteen, but I'm glad it's not me." I smiled at all of them.

"I don't know how you do it," Alex sighed. "I'd hate to be around a bunch of teenagers every single day. That would wear me out."

"Yes," I began, but was interrupted by the waiter.

"The roast chicken?"

"Me," Kevin said.

After the plates were passed around, Alex tapped lightly on his wineglass with his knife.

"A toast," he said.

"What are we toasting, Al?" Kevin asked.

Alex looked at Jean and smiled secretively, the way he always smiled. Jean dropped her eyes and giggled.

"We're going to have a baby."

I caught my breath as Kevin slowly broke out in a grin and pounded Alex lightly on the shoulder.

"That's so great! Congratulations, you guys!"

"Oh, that's wonderful," I added, composing myself quickly. "Are you feeling okay, Jean?"

"Yes, I'm fine. A little sick at the beginning, but I'm nearly three months now, so I'm starting to feel better."

I glanced at Jean's half-full wineglass, and quickly looked away before she could sense my disapproval, but not quickly enough. "Just one little glass," she said and smiled sheepishly.

I felt a wave a nausea rise up from the bottom of my stomach and into my throat, and shakily lifted a hand to push back my hair. My envy and longing were so well formed, so pure in their craving and so astonishingly unexpected, that I was afraid I had spoken them aloud. My bracelet hit my wineglass and knocked it over, and a deep maroon stain spread across the snow-white linen table-cloth, stopping just in front of Kevin. He looked up at me, surprised. I stared at the stain, suddenly enraptured by its beauty, so bold and sensual: the rich red, the free lines of its curves, the little splatters at its edges, the odd way it reached from me to Kevin. Tears stung my eyes. I was embarrassed and kept my head down. "Oh, I'm sorry," I said softly.

"No harm done," Kevin said with unexpected gentleness. He called the waiter over and got a fresh napkin to cover the stain and poured a new glass of wine for me. I smiled at him tentatively but gratefully. He met my eyes and nodded slightly.

"Now, the toast," Alex said gaily. "To a new life!"

"To new parents!" Kevin added.

I lifted my glass, but turned away from Alex and Jean's raw happiness. There was something I should do, I thought. Or something I could have done, that might have prepared me better, that would keep the tears from coming at unpredictable moments in inappropriate company. Surely there was something. Then it came to me, absurd but achingly true. *I should have walked him to the subway.*

I was humbled in front of my food, vulnerable with these sudden strangers, and so I took each bite slowly, heard every word with caution and became silent and still. During coffee, when I noticed Jean's energy flag, and Alex glance at his watch, I breathed a little easier, and relaxed in my chair. It was almost over.

We said our goodbyes on the corner. Kevin and I walked a block in silence before he said agreeably, "That was a nice dinner, don't you think?"

"Yes, lovely," I murmured, and looked up at the sky. You could never see the stars in the city, but I knew they were there, behind the dark and the chill and the artificial glow of streetlights. I walked down the street next to

Kevin, and I turned up my coat collar against the cold and against all the strange events and sudden news I would never be able to predict or prepare for.

THE LAST DAY OF THE YEAR

It is bitterly, maddeningly cold outside my apartment today. I have ventured down Bleecker Street twice; around eleven this morning for bagels for the assorted children who are wedged into my small place, and again around three for sandwiches for these same children, three of which are mine.

I have had Bach playing, and the television, and a headache, and PMS all day. The children want to go ice skating at

Rockefeller Center. I have said no, emphatically, without a trace of guilt, as I took them to the museum and FAO Schwarz yesterday, and it required a subway, a bus, and a taxi with the four of them and a stroller to do so.

They have worn me down, but I was already pretty threadbare. My soon-to-be-ex-husband has sent me roses and sweet peas today, the last day of the year, presumably to sound a positive note that will resonate into the new year for us. In my weakened and exhausted state the gesture takes on epic proportions, and I seriously consider bagging the divorce and asking him to meet me somewhere in a warmer clime.

The apartment is a mess. There is an exhibit at the Museum of Modern Art I am dying to see, but would not consider having these small terrorists accompany me to. This morning they have dropped a chunk of ice off the terrace and onto the sunroof of the Chinese restaurant below, cracking the glass, and I have had to endure a lecture from the owner, who acts as if I had masterminded the attack myself. When I confront the little perpetrators, they reply, with alarming sarcasm, "We're sorry, we're just children." At the moment, I feel the same.

Bach is getting tedious, no more able to summon up his true feelings than I am. Out of the numbing collage of frustration and nostalgia this day has provoked, one image stays acutely in focus, an image on which to hang all the unexplained but painful surges within me. It was when I went out for the sandwiches, with my three-year-old in her billowy purple coat in tow, clutching tightly to my hand and my sleeve.

She has an inexplicable fear of wind, of coats and umbrellas blowing off and away, and nothing I say eases her anxiety. Last summer, on Martha's Vineyard, she became hysterical when a sudden gust carried our beach umbrella across the sand, and I was unable to console her for a very long time.

Today, though there is no wind, she makes certain both our coats are buttoned all the way up, and tightens her grip on my hand as we round the corner and step into the warmth of the Jack and Jill Deli on Carmine Street. She pulls me to the case of sweets and stands with her face pressed to the glass, not wanting them, just waiting. This is the same deli she and I were in when I was robbed, soon after I moved here. We had just been to the grocery, and I had tucked my wallet in my coat pocket as we walked into the store. As I stood at the counter and ordered our sandwiches, a skinny woman in black tights and a ragged sweater bumped me to pick up the menu near my elbow. She glanced at it, then put it down, and quickly walked out. A dark, sweet-faced man handed me my sandwiches, and when I reached for my wallet, I discovered it was gone. I started to cry. "That woman who was just here took my wallet," I whimpered, handing him back the food. He pushed the paper bag back across the counter. "We trust you. You pay when you can." His eyes were soft and fringed with thick lashes. Since then I have gone in for bagels and cappuccino nearly every morning, mostly to see him and his equally adorable partner. There are closer places for coffee, but—they trust me.

Today, as I wait for my food, a tall, blond, and bearded man comes in and asks my friend for coffee and points to a chocolate-glazed cream puff in the case. My friend asks him, "For here or to go?" The blond man again points to the cream puff. My friend motions to the restaurant—"Here?"—and then points outside—"To go?"

The blond man gestures toward the restaurant. My friend, urging him toward the tables, says, "Have a seat." The man looks at him questioningly, then cautiously makes his way to the partner who is making my sandwiches further down the counter, from whom he tries to order the same thing. "I don't think he understood," I say to my friend. He glances at the awkward little scene unfolding and motions a waitress to take care of the customer. The blond man finally takes a seat at the furthest table in the corner of the deli and tries to explain to the waitress what he wants. Then I watch him get up and follow her to the pastry case where I am standing. He indicates the pathetic chocolate cream puff once more, and looks over toward me with shame and sadness. Or maybe it is I who am ashamed and sad. As he returns to his seat, I murmur to my friend, the trusting deli owner, "I feel sorry for someone trying to negotiate New York City with no English. It's hard enough when you do speak the language."

He nods. "That's for sure." But he is not really moved.

I cannot help glancing back at the man in the corner, and I see him devour the cream puff in one huge, intense bite. My heart, which is long since cracked, which is already weighted and worn with the trials of this whole year now passing, squeezes and swells my chest from the inside. My eyes fill, and I herd my little daughter out the door. The frozen air makes the tears bite. My daughter stops, clutches a fold of my coat, and reaches her other hand over to grab my own hand in a tiny, tight embrace. She is

ROSANNE CASH

afraid of the wind. And I am afraid of her fear, and of the millions of possibilities for heartbreak that lie around every corner. We have never been so alone on Bleecker Street.

So, after the Chinese lecture, after the lonely episode in the deli, after the fear of the wind have all subsided, I take the children to SoHo, to the street market at Spring and Wooster, and set them loose with spending money of their own. The baby falls asleep in her stroller, bundled in her Victorian-princess purple coat, and I buy a velvet hat and a pair of silver earrings while I push her slowly around.

We walk back to the West Village through an icy breeze, the twelve-year-olds complaining the entire way, heading for a trattoria in our neighborhood the girls know and love. It is just past six o'clock, and there is only one couple in the restaurant. A bouquet of black and silver balloons is tied in a corner, awaiting the true denizens of New Year's Eve, who won't arrive for several hours. We take a corner table, and I order one glass of red wine, three

Cokes and a Seven-Up. They have a special guest entertainer tonight, this being New Year's Eve, and I hear him mutter amiably to the waiters as he makes his way to the piano, "Jesus, it's only six-thirty." He sings "What Are You Doing On New Year's Eve?" and I indulge in a brief reverie of self-pity. He asks for requests and I send the girls up to request "More Than You Know." He says over the microphone to the crowd, which has swollen slightly by this time, "The request is for 'More Than You Know,' a beautiful song. Aah, we're feeling sentimental as the year draws to a close." You bet we are, mister. More than you know. He performs a slightly histrionic rendition, and I dutifully send the girls up with a tip. The girls request "Sunrise, Sunset" and give him a dollar of their own.

We finish our fettuccine and as we get up to leave, he comes over to thank us and shake our hands. He looks at me with bemusement and glances around at the children. "My, what a lot of girls," he says. God, how I must look to him, and to the other diners in their holiday sequins. A woman in a sweatshirt and velvet hat with four small girls and a stroller and the air of a trail guide as I shield and herd them through New Year's Eve in Greenwich Village. "Yes, we're just a family of women," I smile.

I rent movies for the children, I buy them hats and noisemakers, and I pretend not to notice that they are making fliers that say "Happy New Year. Don't Drink and Drive." "Try to Be Quiet. Someone May Be Sleeping." They plan to toss these edicts from the scene of their earlier crime. I watch Shirley Temple with the baby and I receive phone calls of love and commiseration from beloved faraway friends.

At eleven, with the baby on my lap and the end in sight, I prepare for my annual ritual. I will write on scraps of paper those things—emotional, spiritual, mental, or physical—that have become burdensome, that I wish to leave in the old year, that I wish to bar from the new. I will place them in a bowl and set them on fire, and tomorrow I will throw the ashes in the Hudson River.

I turn over in my mind what I will send up in flames: Fear. Old anger. Resentment and judgment? Addiction to Pain? Inability to Let Go of the Past? Not to mention the ten extra pounds that have clung to my hips and thighs since giving birth to my fearful little princess.

I decide to include the girls in the ritual and call to them to write out on slips of paper their own versions of what they want to cast aside in this waning year. Although there is much rolling of eyes, they eagerly set themselves to the task. We gather around the bowl and read aloud our innermost impediments as we toss them in. One child wants to let go of a boy in her class whom she detests. Two of them want to let go of breaking the sunroof of the Chinese restaurant. I smile; it's nice to see a little well-placed guilt. My oldest wants to let go of being embarrassed that she has "hippie" parents. I wince, but I understand that her father and I are indeed eccentric compared to her friends' parents. I suddenly recall her first Christmas, when she was eleven months old. She had toddled over to the Christmas tree and, unbeknownst to me, had systematically licked all the glitter off the low-hanging ornaments. The next day, when I changed her diaper, her poop was aglow with brilliant little flecks of silver and blue. Now she is twelve, and she has forgotten everything, including who she is. I miss her.

My middle daughter wants to let go of our divorce. I murmur some comment to her that gets lost in the blur of our combined pain, and release a breath I seem to have been holding all day. I toss in my lack of trust, my need to control, and my fear of aging. The baby says she wants to put something in, but doesn't want to tell us what it is. She keeps her own counsel, something I am just beginning to learn. So, we set our anxieties on fire and I open a window and blow the smoke out over Seventh Avenue, and the girls race to the terrace to put a little fear into the heart of our Chinese friend, who glares up at them from the sidewalk below as they hurl their pink paper admonishments over the edge. I let them go. I let him go. I let it all go.